The Boxcar Children Mysteries

THE BOXCAR CHILDREN
SURPRISE ISLAND
THE YELLOW HOUSE MYSTERY
MYSTERY RANCH
MIKE'S MYSTERY
BLUE BAY MYSTERY
THE WOODSHED MYSTERY
THE LIGHTHOUSE MYSTERY
THE MOUNTAIN TOP MYSTERY
SCHOOLHOUSE MYSTERY
CABOOSE MYSTERY
HOUSEBOAT MYSTERY
SNOWBOUND MYSTERY
TREE HOUSE MYSTERY
BICYCLE MYSTERY
MYSTERY IN THE SAND
MYSTERY BEHIND THE WALL
BUS STATION MYSTERY
BENNY UNCOVERS A MYSTERY
THE HAUNTED CABIN
   MYSTERY
THE DESERTED LIBRARY
   MYSTERY
THE ANIMAL SHELTER
   MYSTERY
THE OLD MOTEL MYSTERY
THE MYSTERY OF THE HIDDEN
   PAINTING
THE AMUSEMENT PARK
   MYSTERY
THE MYSTERY OF THE MIXED-
   UP ZOO

THE CAMP-OUT MYSTERY
THE MYSTERY GIRL
THE MYSTERY CRUISE
THE DISAPPEARING FRIEND
   MYSTERY
THE MYSTERY OF THE SINGING
   GHOST
MYSTERY IN THE SNOW
THE PIZZA MYSTERY
THE MYSTERY HORSE
THE MYSTERY AT THE DOG
   SHOW
THE CASTLE MYSTERY
THE MYSTERY OF THE LOST
   VILLAGE
THE MYSTERY ON THE ICE
THE MYSTERY OF THE
   PURPLE POOL
THE GHOST SHIP MYSTERY
THE MYSTERY IN
   WASHINGTON, DC
THE CANOE TRIP MYSTERY
THE MYSTERY OF THE HIDDEN
   BEACH
THE MYSTERY OF THE MISSING
   CAT
THE MYSTERY AT SNOWFLAKE
   INN
THE MYSTERY ON STAGE
THE DINOSAUR MYSTERY
THE MYSTERY OF THE STOLEN
   MUSIC

THE OUTER SPACE MYSTERY

created by
GERTRUDE CHANDLER WARNER

Illustrated by Charles Tang

SCHOLASTIC INC.
New York Toronto London Auckland Sydney

ISBN 0-590-95601-9

12 11 10 9 8 7 6 5 4   8 9/9 0 1 2/0

Printed in the U.S.A.   40

First Scholastic printing, July 1997

Contents

CHAPTER 1

Off Again!

"I can't believe we're going to college!" said Violet Alden, as the van rounded a steep mountain curve.

Next to her, fourteen-year-old Henry Alden grinned. "We're not exactly *going* to college," he teased his little sister. "We'll only be at Mountvale College for five days, for Grandfather's conference."

"Isn't it strange that we were in Connecticut this morning," said twelve-year-old Jessie from the seat behind her sister and brother, "and now we're in the West Virginia mountains!"

"It *is* different here, that's for sure," agreed Randy Merchant, their driver. He had picked up the Aldens at the airport.

"I liked the plane ride," piped Benny, the youngest Alden. "But this ride is fun, too."

Even though the van had several seats, the Alden children sat together. They were used to being close together and had grown to like it. The four children once lived in an abandoned boxcar. That was before their grandfather, James Alden, found them and took them to his big house in Connecticut.

James Alden even had the old boxcar brought to his house so the children could play in it. Grandfather took the Aldens on trips all over the country. The children had solved many mysteries and had some wonderful adventures along the way.

Now Jessie checked the pile of luggage in the back. She counted the suitcases — there were a lot for five people. Jessie liked to keep track of things.

"What are you doing at this conference?" she asked her grandfather. "You told us once, but I forgot."

"I'm the moderator," James Alden replied. "My old friend Able Porter is the president of Mountvale College. He asked me to moderate this conference for young scientists. I introduce the speakers and tell everyone when it's time for lunch."

"I can do that!" exclaimed six-year-old Benny.

Grandfather laughed. "I may need your help. Sometimes scientists become so wrapped up in their work, they don't remember to eat."

"I could *never* forget to eat," said Benny. The others laughed.

"It's so pretty here," said ten-year-old Violet. "I can't wait to take pictures." Violet never went anywhere without her camera.

"Are there wild animals in these woods?" Henry asked the driver. "Like bears and mountain lions?"

Randy steered into another twisting turn.

"There are no mountain lions. But we do have bobcats and black bears."

"I think I see a bear now!" Benny cried, looking through his grandfather's field glasses. "No, it's just an old log."

"Feel the air," Jessie said, her hair blowing in the breeze from the open window. "It's so cool."

"Midsummer is nice in the mountains," Grandfather said. "Back home in Connecticut, it's hot."

"Can we go hiking?" Henry asked Randy. "That looks like a trail over there."

"Hiking, fishing, rock climbing, we've got it all," Randy replied. "But," he added mysteriously, "Stay off *that* trail."

"How come?" Henry asked.

Instead of answering, Randy said, "Wait'll you see our observatory. We've got a twenty-four-inch telescope. It's a beauty," he said proudly, slowing the van. "And here we are!"

The van glided into a wide driveway flanked by stone pillars. At the end of the circular drive were several brick buildings.

The largest had four white columns and an arched front door.

The Aldens tumbled from the van, eager to stretch their legs. Grandfather helped Randy unload their luggage.

A man with iron-gray hair and black-rimmed glasses came through the front door. He hurried down the graveled path, a big smile curving his thick mustache.

"James!" he cried, clasping Grandfather's hand. "It's been too long!"

"Able, it's good to see you," Grandfather said heartily. "May I present my grandchildren — Henry, Jessie, Violet, and Benny. Children, this is my friend Dr. Porter. He is the president of Mountvale College."

The Aldens said hello and shook the man's hand.

"Welcome to Mountvale," greeted Dr. Porter. "I hope your visit will be pleasant. But first let's get you settled. We've put you in the Seneca Building."

Randy scooped up several suitcases and led the way down another graveled path. "Follow me, everybody."

Benches sat invitingly under the trees. Students lolled on the grassy lawn, reading or talking.

A smiling woman with blond hair stood in the doorway of a two-story building.

"Welcome to Mountvale," she said. Jessie noticed the woman's voice had the same soft drawl as Randy's. "I'm Hazel Watson. I'm the housekeeper for this dorm."

"You undoubtedly keep the place running smoothly," said Grandfather.

Hazel laughed. "I try my best. This is the lounge. Feel free to relax here," she said, sweeping through a room with a high ceiling and tall windows. A massive stone fireplace covered an entire wall.

"Boy, I bet you could roast a lot of marshmallows in that!" Benny remarked.

"You must be hungry," Hazel guessed. "There's a cookout this evening for everyone attending the conference. But I've put some fruit in your rooms to tide you over."

As they walked, Hazel pointed to the dining room. "Except on special occasions, like tonight, we eat in there," she said.

They went up a flight of stone steps. Doors with woodburned number plates lined the corridor.

"I've put you girls in number six," said Hazel, opening a door. "You boys are next door. Mr. Alden is down here." She and Grandfather continued to the end of the hall.

Randy deposited the Aldens' suitcases in their rooms.

"How come we can't use that trail?" Henry asked. "The one you told us to stay away from."

Randy acted as if he didn't hear. "I've got to go fetch the rest of the bags," he said as he hurried down the steps.

"I wonder why he won't tell us about the trail," Henry said, opening his suitcase on the floor of their room.

Benny crunched into a crispy apple he found in a basket on the dresser. "You know what I think? I think we're off on another adventure!"

Just then Jessie and Violet knocked on the boys' door.

When the girls came in, Violet glanced around the room. Twin beds were made up with woven bedspreads. Photographs of misty mountains hung on the walls.

"Our room looks just like this," she remarked.

"Except you've got clothes on the floor," Jessie said. She had already unpacked and put her clothes in the bureau. She hated living out of a suitcase, even for a few days.

Henry gazed out the tall windows to the lawn below. "Looks like they're setting up for the cookout."

Benny tossed his apple core into the trash. "I wonder if they need some help."

"You just want to sample everything!" Henry said, laughing. "Let's see if Grandfather wants to go down now."

Jessie took out the room key. "Let me go lock our door."

"The doors lock automatically," Henry pointed out. "Just pull it closed."

Grandfather wanted to shower before going to the cookout. "Go ahead," he urged. "I'll be down in about twenty minutes."

The children hurried down the stone steps and out the side door.

Tables covered with yellow-striped cloths ringed the lawn. Randy and another man were barbequing chicken and hamburgers over a smoking grill. A cart with pitchers of iced tea stood next to an ice-filled tub of sodas.

"I'm thirsty," said Benny.

"I'll ask Randy if we can have a soda," said Jessie, heading toward the grill.

"Make way!" yelled someone from behind her.

A dark-haired young woman hurried by, carrying a huge tray of cheese and pickles.

"I'll help you put that down," Benny offered, his thirst forgotten. He hoped he'd be rewarded with a pickle.

"No problem," said the girl, quickly arranging the platters. "I've got to set up before the crowd arrives."

Already young men wearing ties and young women in flowered summer dresses milled about on the lawn. Everyone wore name tags.

Hazel Watson came over to the Aldens.

"Here are your name tags," she said, pinning a plastic square to Benny's shirt.

The dark-haired girl bustled past again, this time carrying a huge bowl of chips.

"Rachel," Hazel said, halting the girl. "There are no cups with the drinks."

"Yes, Mrs. Watson," Rachel replied, sounding frustrated. "I'll fetch them on the next trip."

A young man stopped to read Benny's name tag. "Hello, Benny Alden. I'm Mark Jacobs. Pleased to meet you." He shook Benny's hand, then smiled at the other children.

"Are you a student here?" Jessie asked. She thought the young man had wonderful brown eyes.

"Yes," Mark replied. "I'm studying astronomy. In fact, I'm presenting a paper at the conference."

"What's it about?" asked Henry.

Mark lowered his voice to a whisper. "My secret discovery!" he said, wiggling his eyebrows.

Violet giggled. "Astronomy is about the stars, right?"

Mark nodded. "And the moon and planets and the sun."

Just then Randy Merchant rang a bell. "Time to eat," he bellowed to the guests.

Everyone formed a line. Henry was extra-hungry. He took a hamburger and a big piece of chicken.

A pudgy young man behind him took a hamburger. "The food in this place isn't that great," he complained. His badge read EUGENE SCOTT.

Henry introduced himself to Eugene. "My grandfather is the moderator of the conference. Are you studying astronomy like Mark Jacobs?"

"I'm a better astronomer than Jacobs is *any* day," Eugene said scornfully, leaving the food line.

Henry shrugged. Maybe the guy was just cranky because he was hungry.

The Aldens found a small table under a tree. Grandfather sat with Dr. Porter at a bigger table.

Mark Jacobs brought his plate over. "May I join you?"

"Sure," said Benny. He liked the young astronomer.

"Eat fast," said Mark, looking up at the dark clouds. "I'm afraid we're in for a real mountain thunderstorm."

Rachel walked by with a pitcher of iced tea. "Refills?"

Mark held out his glass. "The food is really good."

"At least *you* don't have to work for it," she said, stalking away.

"Who is she?" asked Violet.

"That's Rachel Cunningham," Mark replied. "She's from the little town at the bottom of the mountain."

"Is she a student, too?" Henry wanted to know.

Mark nodded. "Yes, but she works as a waitress and a maid to help earn tuition money. Rachel is — "

But before he could finish, it began to rain — big, splattering drops followed by daggers of lightning!

CHAPTER 2

The Cabin in the Glen

Jessie grabbed Benny's hand and ran toward the dormitory. Lightning flashed all around them. The claps of thunder were deafening.

Everyone scurried for shelter. Jessie and Benny raced inside the Seneca Building, just ahead of Violet and Henry. Mark Jacobs was right behind them.

A fire blazed in the huge stone fireplace. Several people gathered around the warmth of the flames.

"I am so wet!" cried Violet as she plopped

down on the hearth to dry off. "Those rain-drops were cold!"

"That was a mountain cloudburst," said Mark, wringing out his soggy tie. "Definitely not a gentle summer shower."

Thunder rocked the building.

Benny's eyes grew round. "This storm is very noisy," he said, trying to be brave.

"It'll be over soon," Mark assured him. "One thing about weather up here — it changes quickly. If it's clear tomorrow night, I'll let you look through the telescope."

"Can we see Jupiter?" asked Henry.

"Sure," said Mark. "I wish I could show you Saturn, too. But it rises much later. You'd have to get up very early in the morning, while it's still dark out."

"I always get up really early," Benny bragged. The storm was rumbling down the mountain and he felt braver.

"But first you have to go to bed," said a familiar voice.

"Grandfather," said Violet. "Where were you?"

"Able Porter and I waited out the rain in the main building. But before we got there we were soaked," replied James Alden. "I'm going to toast by the fire a bit. You children should go on up to bed. You've had a busy day."

After saying good night, the Aldens went upstairs. Jessie and Violet unlocked their door and went into room six.

Henry got out the key to his and Benny's room.

"It's already open," whispered Benny. He pushed on the door, which swung inward. "Maybe somebody's in there!"

"Let me go in first," Henry cautioned. He stepped carefully into the room, switching on the light.

First he checked under the beds and then in the tiny bathroom. But no one was hiding.

"All clear," Henry told Benny.

"Who was in our room?" Benny asked.

"I don't know," Henry replied. "But I know the door was locked. Somebody came in while we were at the cookout. Is anything missing?"

"Hey!" cried Benny. "There were four apples in the basket. I ate one. But look!" He held up two apples. "Somebody took an apple."

A sharp rap on the doorjam caused them both to jump.

Hazel Watson came into the room. "I heard your conversation from the hall. Is anything wrong?"

"Somebody broke into our room," Henry told her. "We found the door unlocked."

"Oh, dear," said the housekeeper. "I hope nothing is missing."

"An apple," Benny reported.

"Are you *sure* the door was locked, Henry?" Hazel asked. "People have been arriving for the conference all evening. Maybe one of them accidently went into your room."

Now Henry wasn't so certain. "Maybe I was wrong," he said. "Sorry to bother you."

"No trouble. See you in the morning,"

Hazel said, pulling the door shut behind her.

Henry went over to the window to close the blinds. Suddenly he slipped and nearly fell.

There was a puddle of water beneath the window.

"Water!" he exclaimed. "How did that get here?"

Then it came to him. Whoever had broken into their room might have been at the cookout. Drenched from the storm, the intruder had dripped on the floor.

Benny bent down. "What is this?" He held up a damp, pale blue piece of paper.

"It looks like a gum or candy wrapper," Henry observed. "The person must have dropped it."

"You know what this means?" Benny exclaimed. "We have a new mystery to solve!"

The next morning was sparkling and sunny. The rain had left the campus fresh and green.

In the dining room, the Aldens sat at a

table by a big window. The room buzzed with the chatter of scientists. Grandfather was attending a special breakfast meeting.

Violet put down her menu. "Ugh! Who'd want mountain trout for *breakfast*?"

"Fresh-caught trout is supposed to be good," Henry said. "But I'm with you, Violet. I can't face fish this early."

Rachel Cunningham came over to take their orders. She wore a cheerful pink sweater, but no smile.

Jessie wondered why the girl seemed so unhappy. It was a beautiful day. Who could be glum under such blue skies?

Jessie smiled at Rachel when she brought the Aldens' orders, but Rachel didn't respond.

While the Aldens spooned up oatmeal with maple syrup and raisins, they discussed the new mystery.

"You should have shown the puddle and that wrapper to Hazel," Jessie said to Henry. "That's proof somebody was in your room."

"Hazel had already left," Henry said.

"Anyway, she thinks someone just went in there by accident."

"If the person didn't take anything, maybe it *was* an accident," Violet mused.

Benny waved his spoon. "They took one of my apples!"

"I guess he — or she — was hungry," said Henry.

"But he couldn't have been hungry if he'd just come in from the cookout," Jessie pointed out.

Henry buttered a corn muffin. "We don't know for sure that the person was at the cookout. Maybe he just got caught in the storm."

Just then Randy Merchant walked by, carrying a Styrofoam cup of juice. "Hey, guys!" he greeted. "When you finish, come by the observatory. I'll show you the telescope."

"Oh, boy!" Benny said, stuffing half a muffin in his mouth. "Let's hurry!"

Violet laughed. "Benny! The telescope isn't going anywhere." But she was eager to visit the observatory, too.

"Good breakfast," Jessie said when Rachel cleared their plates. "Thanks."

"Don't thank me," she said shortly. "I'm not the cook."

As the Aldens went outside, Jessie remarked, "I wonder why Rachel is so unfriendly."

"Maybe she's just having a bad day." Henry indicated a sign beside a graveled path. "The observatory is this way."

The trail wound upward, between jagged rocks and thick bushes. The children were out of breath when, a while later, they reached a windowless building capped by a white dome.

"We're on the very top of the mountain," said Henry as they headed toward the building. "You can see the campus down there."

They opened the door to the building and walked down a hall lined with desks and bookcases. At the end of the hall another door stood open.

"Come in!" Randy's voice echoed from within.

The children stepped into a huge round room. The ceiling curved overhead like the inside of an egg. In the center of the room was a large cylinder-shaped object.

Randy Merchant stood at the base of the instrument, holding a pair of pliers. "Welcome," he said, grinning.

Henry looked up, marveling at the enormous structure. "We're inside the dome, aren't we?"

"There's a big crack in it," Benny said, pointing to a narrow slit in the roof. "You should get it fixed."

Randy laughed. "The slit is supposed to be there. The roof slides open when the telescope is in use." He patted the huge cylinder. "I told you it was a beauty."

"Can we look through it?" asked Benny.

"I'm doing some maintenance on it right now," Randy replied. "But I'll tell you about it. This is a twenty-four-inch reflecting telescope."

"How does it work?" asked Henry. He was interested in mechanical devices.

Randy adjusted a wheel on the side of the

telescope. "There are two types of telescopes," he explained. "Refracting and reflecting. Both types gather light and send it toward the eye of the viewer. Refracting telescopes use a lens. Reflecting telescopes use a mirror. Both types of lenses allow you to see objects very far away."

"Speaking of far away, why is this building so far from the rest of the college?" Jessie wanted to know.

"Good question," said Randy. "Observatories are always located in high places, like a mountaintop. The air is clearer up here and we are farther away from city lights. You want a really dark sky so you can see the stars."

Henry touched the sleek white metal of the telescope. "Are you an astronomer like Mark Jacobs and Eugene Scott?"

"Oh, you've met those two already," Randy said with a chuckle. "No, I'm not a student. I work for the college, keeping the telescope in working order. I'm also a writer," he added proudly.

"I'm a writer, too," Benny put in. "I can

write my name. I can write Watch's name, too."

"Watch is our dog back home," Jessie told Randy. "What have you written?"

Randy went over to a desk and pulled out a box.

"These are my journals," he said. "I write down everything the astronomers do. Even what they eat for snacks. Mark likes peanut butter sandwiches. Eugene Scott eats anything. I hope to get an article published about young astronomers in a science magazine."

Henry glanced at the clock over the desk. "This has been great, but we should let you get back to work."

"Come back tonight," Randy urged. "Mark will show you the stars like you've never seen them."

The Aldens went back outside and down the mountain. It was too early for lunch. They decided to walk through the campus and down the main drive.

"Here's that trail we saw on the way in," said Henry.

"But Randy told us to stay away from it," Violet said.

"But he wouldn't say *why*," said Benny.

"I'm sure he has a good reason — " Jessie began, but a thrashing noise in the woods cut her off.

The children caught a glimpse of a small animal running down the trail.

"What was that?" Violet exclaimed.

"Let's follow it and find out!" Henry cried.

They hiked a while, swatting gnats and looking for the animal they'd seen. Then the trail became narrower and fainter until it disappeared altogether.

"I think we should go back," Jessie said.

"I do, too," agreed Henry. "But which way is back?"

Violet gazed down into the hollow. "Is that a chimney?" she said to the others. "It must belong to a cabin."

Jessie stared at the stone chimney. "I don't remember any cabin near the college. I think we're lost!"

CHAPTER 3

Pictures in the Sky

"We shouldn't have gone down this trail," Violet said. "No one knows where we are."

"Don't worry. We'll find our way back," Henry assured her.

"I'm hungry," Benny said. Lost or not, he wasn't about to miss lunch. Looking around, he spotted a faint path twisting through the trees. "I think this is it!"

"Benny, you're right!" Jessie gave him a quick hug.

The children hurried through the dense

underbrush. Soon the narrow track widened into the main driveway. Within minutes, they were back on the campus of Mountvale College.

Streams of people poured from the main building.

"Just in time for lunch," Henry said. "The conference must be over for the morning."

"And there's Grandfather," Violet exclaimed, running over to him. "Grandfather, are you eating with us?"

"I'm sorry, Violet. I've been asked to sit with today's guest speakers," James Alden replied. "You children go ahead. I'll see you later this evening."

The Aldens entered the dining room and quickly staked out a table. Rachel Cunningham brought over four menus.

Jessie tried to be friendly. "Hi, Rachel. How are you doing?"

"Fair," replied the young woman. She popped her chewing gum impatiently. "What'll it be?"

Jessie hadn't even had time to read the

menu. She noticed a group of students at the next table. They were snapping their fingers at Rachel.

"I think those people over there want you," she said. "You can take their order first."

Rachel barely glanced in their direction. "Rich kids," she said with a sniff. "Just because their parents have a lot of money doesn't mean they can treat me like a maid."

"Hey, Rachel," called one of the young men. "What's good today?"

"I don't cook the food," she said over her shoulder. "I just serve it." Then she took an order pad and pencil from her skirt pocket.

Benny noticed the big ring of keys attached to her belt. "You sure have a lot of keys," he said admiringly. "Do you know what they all go to?"

"I should," Rachel replied with a sigh. "I have to clean each of those rooms every day."

"You have keys to all the dorm rooms?" Henry asked, suddenly interested.

"All the rooms in the Seneca Building,"

she said. "Now, what do you want for lunch?"

Henry ordered a chicken salad sandwich with potato chips and milk. So did everyone else.

When Rachel left, Henry leaned forward. "She has keys to all the rooms," he said. "Rachel could have been the one in our room last night. She was at the cookout. And she got caught in the storm."

"I was thinking the same thing," said Jessie. "But why would Rachel break into your room? Was she looking for something? Nothing was taken."

"One of my apples," Benny reminded her.

Violet smiled. "That's not a very big crime, Benny. Maybe Rachel didn't have anything to eat at the cookout and she was hungry."

"But why break into our room to steal an apple?" Henry asked. "She works near the kitchen — she could have anything she wants."

"Henry's right," Jessie agreed. "It doesn't

really make sense. Rachel's kind of touchy, but I think she's okay, deep down inside."

"I don't think it's Rachel, either," Violet said.

"Well, even if it doesn't make sense, right now she's our number one suspect," said Henry.

Just then their lunches came. The children were so hungry that they didn't speak until there were only potato chip crumbs on their plates.

The students were leaving. It was time for the afternoon session to begin.

As the Aldens were getting up, they saw Eugene Scott pull his chair out in front of a group heading for the door. Mark Jacobs was hit by the chair.

"Sorry," Eugene said.

Mark rubbed his shin. "It's okay. It was an accident."

But Henry wasn't so sure. To him, it looked as if Eugene had done it on purpose.

Then Eugene hurried out of the dining room with a triumphant smirk on his face.

Mark waved to the Aldens. "Hey, are you

guys coming to the observatory tonight? The sky should be perfect."

"We'll be there," Jessie answered. She was excited about looking through the big telescope.

"Will we see the moon?" Benny wanted to know. He didn't believe the moon was made of Swiss cheese, but he wanted to make sure.

"You bet," Mark said. "There are many secrets in the heavens. I might even show you mine!"

With that, he disappeared into the crowd.

At the reception desk, Henry picked up a map showing the trails around the campus.

"The trail we were on isn't marked," he said.

"But we know it's there," said Violet. "Maybe it's an old trail nobody is supposed to use anymore."

Jessie had been thinking. "It's almost like that trail is a secret."

"Another mystery to solve!" Benny crowed. "We're going to be busy this week!"

*   *   *

The evening was cool and clear wh Aldens hiked up the trail to the observatory. Frogs cheeped and crickets chirped along the path. An owl hooted in the distance.

"Whoever said the woods were quiet?" Violet remarked. She was glad when they reached the white building at the top. The owl's eerie cry made her a little jumpy.

Randy Merchant met them at the door.

"I'm on my way out," he told them. "Mark is at the 'scope. He's expecting you."

He climbed into the school van parked on the side of a narrow road. People who didn't want to walk the trail could drive up the road instead.

Inside the observatory, the dome was open, allowing the huge telescope to poke into the night sky.

Mark Jacobs stood at the top of a set of rolling metal stairs, adjusting some knobs on the telescope.

"Hi!" he said as he waved them toward the stairs. "Come on up."

"These steps won't move, will they?" Jessie wondered nervously.

"The wheels have brakes," Mark told her. "It's safe."

One by one, the children climbed up onto the platform.

Mark moved away from the eyepiece. "Who wants to see Jupiter?"

"I do!" Benny said eagerly. Then he asked, "What's Jupiter?"

"Jupiter is the largest planet in our solar system," Mark replied. He positioned Benny beneath the eyepiece. "Now, look through there. Do you see a yellowish sphere with grayish stripes?"

Benny stared a moment. Then he cried, "Yes, I do! It's got a red dot in the center!"

The others took turns peering through the eyepiece.

"Wow!" Henry said, awed. "It looks so close."

"It isn't," Mark said. "It takes Jupiter twelve years to orbit the sun. It's that far away! Our solar system is made up of several planets that orbit the sun."

"Like Mars," Violet continued. "And Venus."

"Can we see the moon?" Benny asked.

Mark shook his head. "Not yet. Moonrise will be in a little while."

Violet thought *moonrise* was a beautiful word. She gazed at the sky through the open roof. "There are a zillion stars when you look through the telescope. I can see a lot with just my eyes, but not that many."

"You can see about two thousand stars on a clear night," Mark said. "The telescope allows us to see hundreds of thousands more."

"I want to see outer space!" Benny declared.

Mark laughed. "You're looking at it! Here's something else — just wait until I bring it into focus." He pushed some buttons. The telescope made a whirring sound as it moved very slightly.

This time Jessie looked first. "I don't see anything."

"Look to your left," Mark instructed. "See that bright cluster of stars?"

"Oh!" she said. "They're so pretty — like jewels."

"That's what they are called," Mark said. "The Jewel Box. If you saw the cluster with the unaided eye, it would appear to be a hazy spot."

While the others viewed the Jewel Box, Mark told them more about stars. "Before man invented the telescope, he used to stare at the sky. He connected the spaces between the stars with imaginary lines and made pictures of animals or objects. Those pictures are called constellations."

Now Mark pushed another button. The dome slowly opened wider, revealing more of the night sky.

"There's a constellation," Henry said. "The Big Dipper." He pointed to the ladle-shaped group of stars in the north.

"I don't see it," Benny said.

"It's right up there," Violet told him. "It looks like a cup with a bent handle."

"The Big Dipper is a good constellation to know," said Mark. "The two outer stars of the cup point to the North Star. If you keep the North Star in your sight, you'll always know which direction you're going."

At that moment, footsteps rang on the hardwood floor.

"Is the lecture over, Jacobs?" said a familiar voice.

Mark leaned over the railing. "Hey, Eugene," he said to the figure standing at the base of the rolling stairs. "Have you met the Aldens?"

"I've seen them around," Eugene said moodily. "You're on my time, Mark."

Mark looked at the clock. "I still have two hours."

"No, you don't," Eugene argued. "It's my turn at the telescope."

"Astronomers sign up for time," Mark explained to the children. "We can only work at night, so we sign up a day ahead. But I'm positive I signed up for this block of time."

Eugene tapped a notebook on the desk against the wall. "Check Randy's log if you don't believe me."

"I will." Mark took the stairs two at a time. The children followed. At the desk, they all stared at the notebook.

Henry read the entry. "It says, 'Eugene Scott, nine till twelve.' "

Mark shook his head. "I can't believe I made such a mistake. . . . Well, you kids can stay. The moon will be rising soon. I know Benny wants to see it."

Eugene clattered up the metal stairs. "I've got important work to do. I can't babysit."

"It's time for us to go anyway," Henry said to Mark. "Thanks for letting us look through the telescope."

It was obvious Eugene Scott didn't want them around.

Outside they saw a dashing red sports car in the parking lot.

"That's Eugene's car," Mark said, as he walked the Aldens down the trail. "He rarely walks up here."

It wasn't until they were in their dorm room that Henry realized something.

Mark Jacobs hadn't shown them his secret discovery.

CHAPTER 4

The Haunted Mountain

Right after breakfast the next morning, the Aldens marched up the mountain to the observatory.

"I think we should take another look at that log," said Jessie. "There was something odd about the way Eugene Scott made Mark leave. Mark said it was *his* turn."

"Mark was so sure he put down the right time," Henry agreed.

An early morning mist drifted among the trees like ghostly scarves.

"It's spooky up here," Violet said in a

soft voice. "Listen to how quiet it is."

She was right. No birds sang. Not even a small breeze ruffled the treetops.

"It *is* creepy," Jessie agreed.

Henry caught his sister's hand. "I know what you mean."

"Do you mean creepy like ghosts?" Benny's eyes grew round. "Is this mountain haunted?"

"No, it's not," Henry hastily replied, not wanting to frighten his little brother. "It's just so quiet."

At the top of the mountain, the Aldens saw that the parking lot was empty.

"Nobody's here," said Benny.

"Let's try the door anyway." Jessie went up to the front door and turned the handle. "Hello?" she called down the corridor. "Anybody here?"

"Just us mice!" boomed Randy's voice. He came out of his office, a clipboard in one hand.

"We didn't know anyone was here," Henry said. "Your van isn't out front."

"Sometimes I walk up the mountain. Try

to get a little exercise. What can I do for you folks?"

Violet spoke up. "We wondered if we could take a look at that log — the one the astronomers sign to use the telescope. Last night Eugene came in and said Mark was using his time."

"I heard about that," Randy said, leading them to the sign-in desk. "I've never had two scientists sign up for the same clock of time, not since I've been keeping the log." He opened the notebook.

"There it is." Violet pointed to last night's entry. "It *does* say Eugene Scott."

Jessie bent her head closer. "But look — see those marks? It looks like somebody erased a name and wrote Eugene's name over it."

Randy studied the page. "Hmmm. You could be right, Jessie. Mark's name might have been erased. But I don't know when this could have happened. I'm here all day."

"Maybe one of the students came in early to change the names," Henry suggested.

Randy shook his head. "Astronomers

rarely get up early. They stay up all night working in the observatory. They usually sleep late."

As they left, Henry had a thought. Randy was the log keeper. *He* could have changed the names.

On their way into the dining room for lunch, Jessie stopped to read a poster.

" 'Party time! Join us for the Perseid meteor shower, tomorrow night in the observatory,' " she read aloud.

"What kind of a party is that?" Benny asked.

"Oh, I think you should go," a voice said behind them. Mark ruffled Benny's hair. "They're meteors. Falling stars!"

They found a table by the window. Once more, Mark sat with them.

"Actually, falling stars are not stars at all, but stone fragments," Mark went on. "When these fragments break through our atmosphere, they leave a tail of light. It's like watching fireworks."

Just then Grandfather came in. He pulled

up a chair. "I finally got a break from the conference. May I join you?"

"Please do, Mr. Alden," Mark said. "I was just telling your grandchildren about the upcoming meteor shower."

"We're going to see falling stars!" Violet said. "Can we stay up that late?"

"Absolutely," Grandfather promised. "It isn't every day you get to see a meteor shower from an observatory."

Rachel Cunningham came by with menus. When everyone had ordered, she bustled off, but left the menus on the table.

When she came back with a tray full of drinks, Jessie handed her the menus. "You forgot these," she said.

"I don't know where my mind is today," Rachel said. Then she began passing the drinks.

"I didn't want Coke," Benny told her. "I ordered ginger ale."

"And I'm afraid I didn't ask for iced tea," Grandfather said apologetically.

Rachel hastily snatched up the wrong drinks. "That's right — you said you wanted lemonade. I'll be right back." She hurried away, nearly tripping over another diner.

"She seems awfully nervous," Jessie observed.

"I can see why," Grandfather said. "It's a lot of extra work for her, taking care of conference people and the summer-school students at the same time."

"Still," Mark put in, "Rachel volunteered for the job."

This time Rachel returned with a tray overloaded with the right drinks and their entrees.

Henry saw the tray dip dangerously and jumped up to help but it was too late.

Grandfather's tossed salad landed upside down in his lap.

"Oh, no!" Rachel stood rooted to the floor, her gray eyes horrified. "Look what I've done!"

Grandfather plucked a radish off his shirt. "It's all right, dear girl. Not to worry. I'll go up to my room and change." Trying to make her feel better, he joked, "I *did* ask for a tossed salad."

"You don't understand!" Rachel cried. "I've ruined everything!" Wheeling around, she flung the tray on an empty table and ran across the room.

Jessie started after her. "Rachel! Come back!"

But Rachel was already out the door.

Jessie stared at Henry. "I've never seen anyone so nervous."

Henry nodded. "I wonder what could be bothering her."

The children spent the afternoon exploring the stream that ran alongside the campus. Jessie showed Benny how to make boats out of sticks and leaves. Violet and Henry took pictures of the scenery.

"These should be good enough to enter in a contest," Henry told Violet. "You've got some really nice shots."

Benny launched a fleet of leaf boats down the rushing creek. "Here comes the navy!" he cried gleefully.

Henry measured the progress of the sun over the treetops. "We'd better head back. It's nearly dinnertime."

Scooping his "navy" from the water, Benny neatly lined up the soggy boats on a sandbar. "I'm ready now," he declared. "I'm starving."

"Dinner is supposed to be another picnic," Jessie said. "I wonder if Rachel will be there."

They found out later, when the conference people were gathered once more on the lawn. Rachel Cunningham was rushing between groups, serving drinks. Jessie noticed the young woman's eyes were red-rimmed.

"At least we can eat when we want to," Benny said. The long tables were laden with an assortment of cold dishes, breads, and salads. The dessert table made Benny's eyes pop.

"Hey, there!" Eugene Scott bounded up to the children. "Haven't seen you around today. What have you been up to?"

Henry was surprised by the young man's sudden friendliness. "We've been busy," he said.

"That's good!" Eugene said jovially. "Are

you coming to the closing ceremony on the last day of the conference?"

"I don't know," Jessie replied. "Grandfather hasn't mentioned anything about it."

"You should come," Eugene said. "I want *everybody* to come. I've made a terrific discovery! The world will find out what it is that day!"

"Mark has a discovery, too," Benny put in.

A cloud seemed to drop over Eugene's eyes. "You can believe that my discovery is a thousand times better than his!" With that, he stomped off.

Violet shook her head. "Boy, he's kind of weird."

Jessie pointed to a stage that had been set up near the trees. "There's Rachel with a guitar. I bet she's going to sing! Let's go listen."

After a brief introduction by Dr. Porter, Rachel stood before a microphone.

"Tonight," she said shyly, "I'm going to sing a ballad my granddaddy taught me. The song was passed down from his granddaddy, so it's really old."

She strummed the guitar a few times, then began to sing. Jessie had never heard such a sweet, lilting voice. The words told a story of a family who had to leave their mountain home forever.

When Rachel was through, everyone applauded. Bowing briefly, the young woman left the stage, brushing away compliments from the guests.

"I wish I could sing like that," Violet commented to Jessie later, when they were in their dorm room.

"Rachel is like these mountains. She seems different every day," Jessie mused, pulling down the covers.

Later on, after the girls had fallen asleep, they heard a knock at the door.

It was Hazel Watson, the housekeeper.

"Have you seen Rachel?" she asked the girls. "I can't find her anywhere!"

CHAPTER 5

Where Is Rachel?

"What do you mean you can't find her?" Violet asked.

"She's not in her room," Hazel said. "I just went in there to thank her for singing for us tonight. Her bed is still made up. She's nowhere to be seen, and it's getting very late."

"Maybe she's taking a walk," Violet suggested. "She'll probably come in later."

Hazel shook her head. "Rachel is usually in her room studying as soon as the evening meal is over. This isn't like her at all."

"We'll probably find out tomorrow where she went," Jessie said reassuringly. But she was concerned, too. Rachel had seemed so upset earlier.

When Hazel left, Jessie went over to the window. A thick canopy of trees blocked most of the stars, but a thin, silver moon rose in the east. Was Rachel Cunningham out there somewhere?

Violet always knew when her big sister was worried. "Rachel's from these mountains," she said. "She'll be all right. I'm sure she'll show up tomorrow."

"I hope so," said Jessie, turning away from the window.

The next morning, Rachel had not returned, and the whole campus knew she was missing.

Grandfather spoke briefly to the children just outside the dining hall. "I'm running the entire conference now," he told them. "Able Porter has his hands full with the disappearance of that young woman."

At that moment a sheriff's car wheeled into the circular driveway. A stocky man in a brown uniform and hat climbed out and went inside the administration building.

"Able is probably giving the sheriff a full report," Grandfather said. He checked his watch. "I'd better run. The seminar starts in four minutes."

Benny walked over to the sheriff's car. He admired the golden badge painted on the side. When he grew up, he wanted a car just like this.

"I wonder what's going to happen," Violet said. "How will they ever find one person in these mountains?" She waved at the vast territory surrounding the campus.

The sheriff came outside again, followed by Able Porter and Randy Merchant. The men looked worried.

Mark Jacobs saw the group as he crossed the campus and ran over. He, too, looked concerned.

From where the children were standing, they could hear the men talking.

"I hear you're forming a search party," Mark said to the sheriff.

"That's right," said the officer. "We're

afraid she might be lost in these woods. We need all the help we can get if we want to cover these woods by nightfall."

Jessie shuddered. She remembered the wild animals Randy had mentioned that lived in the woods.

"We can help," Henry said.

The sheriff looked at him dubiously. "We're grateful for your offer, young man, but we need people who know these hills. We don't need someone else getting lost."

"We can do other things," Benny said. "Like talk on walkie-talkies." Next to owning a car with a gold badge on it, Benny longed to have a set of walkie-talkies.

"Benny is right," said Mark. "We'll need radio contact here. If we're all out searching, who will we report in to? Dr. Porter has enough on his hands, running this college. I trust these children."

"Okay!" the sheriff said, happy to have a few more helpers.

The seminar was dismissed for the day

and a search party was organized. The people would work in teams so no one would get lost. Team leaders were issued walkie-talkies, maps, water, and food.

Randy Merchant showed the Aldens how to use the radio equipment in the main office. Then they all went back outside again to see the search party off.

As the teams were about to leave, Mark looked around.

"Where's Eugene Scott?" he asked. "I haven't seen him all day."

"I bet I know where he is," Randy answered in disgust. "In the kitchen."

Mark suddenly looked furious. He stalked into the dining hall and came out a moment later with Eugene.

"What do you need me for?" Eugene was saying defensively. "You have plenty of people to search."

"*Everyone* has volunteered," Mark said, tight-lipped. "Even the children. The Aldens are manning the radios."

Reluctantly, Eugene loaded up with gear.

When the searchers finally headed into the deep woods, Eugene trailed behind. He clearly did not want to go.

"What's with him?" Violet wondered. "You'd think he'd want to help."

"Maybe he's afraid of bears and wildcats," said Benny, as they walked back into the main office.

They settled at the desk in front of the radio equipment. Jessie flipped on the switches. Static crackled from the speakers, so they knew the system was operating.

Henry stationed himself in front of the microphone, ready to receive the first message.

"I wonder if there's any good food in the kitchen," Benny wondered wistfully. "We didn't have much to eat this morning."

It was true. Everyone on the college staff was upset over Rachel's disappearance. Breakfast had been a skimpy meal of cereal and fruit.

As if she heard his comment, Hazel Watson came to the door. She looked worried. "Have you heard anything yet?" she asked the children.

Henry shook his head. "Nothing. But the searchers only left a little while ago."

Hazel heaved a sigh. "I have a problem," she said. "I'm hoping you children can help me."

"We'll be glad to, if we can," said Violet.

"I'm short-handed in the dining room," Hazel said. "With Rachel gone, I have no waitress."

Jessie guessed what was coming next. "You want us to fill in for Rachel?"

"Only during breakfast," Hazel explained. "I've arranged to have buffet-style lunches and dinners. But the conference people expect a hot, served breakfast. I'll be happy to pay you. What do you think?"

"Do I get to carry one of those big trays?" Benny asked eagerly.

Hazel laughed. "No, I have a special job for you, Benny. Rolling silverware into napkins. Can you do that?"

"You bet!" Anything that put him closer to the kitchen was fine with him.

Jessie and Henry looked at each other.

Violet grinned. "We'll do it!" she said.

"And you don't have to pay us," Henry told Hazel.

"Except a snack once in a while," Benny put in.

Hazel laughed. "It's only for one day, the final day of the conference. After that, Rachel — " Her blue eyes were suddenly sad.

Violet patted the older woman on the knee. "Don't worry. They'll find Rachel soon."

But the radio was silent the rest of the morning. At noon, Able Porter came in to relieve the Aldens.

"Go have lunch," he told them. "And then go outside for a walk. It's a beautiful day. You shouldn't let our problems ruin your vacation."

"We don't mind," Jessie told him. "We like Rachel a lot. We want to do anything we can to help find her."

Dr. Porter smiled ruefully. "I'm sure Rachel would be glad to know she has such loyal friends."

As Hazel had promised, lunch was a buffet, with a choice of cold salads, meats, cheeses, and relishes. Everybody served themselves.

The dining room was nearly empty. Most of the conference attendees and all of the summer students were out searching the woods.

Grandfather stopped by the children's table. Violet begged him to eat with them.

He held up a tray filled with sandwiches. "I'm afraid I have to entertain the guest speakers over there. They understand why the seminars are being postponed, but I still can't leave them alone."

"We're manning the radios," said Benny proudly.

"We're on a break right now because Dr. Porter is handling the radios," Jessie explained. "I wonder if he's had any calls."

"I'm sure the searchers are doing everything they can," said Grandfather. "Let's hope they find that young woman before nightfall."

When he left, Violet stared at Jessie. "I never thought of that! Rachel might be in the woods again tonight. It must be so scary!"

"Then what are we sitting here for?" Henry asked. "Instead of taking a walk, let's go look for her!"

The children cleared their table and rushed outside.

Jessie pointed toward the main trails. "Most of the team went that way."

"And some others went up there," Henry said, nodding toward the observatory above them.

"What about that trail we found?" Violet suggested. "The one that's not on the map."

"Good idea," Henry said. "We'll head in that direction."

Today the woods were hot and muggy. Not a leaf stirred. But gnats and mosquitoes provided plenty of activity.

"Next time, bring bug spray," Benny said, slapping his neck.

Violet was in the lead. "Here's where we lost the trail before."

Sure enough, the faint path seemed to disappear into the woods. But the children had broken enough branches the last time to mark the way.

"Look, there's the stone chimney," said Henry. "Let's go check out that cabin."

Jessie led the way down the twisting path. "Maybe Rachel is in there!"

Going down the steep mountainside was hard. Branches smacked them. Benny tripped over a root. Once Jessie thought she saw a snake, but it was only a thick vine.

At last they stumbled into a clearing.

The log cabin was cloaked in shadows. The sky was scraps of blue between tall trees.

The stone chimney jutted crookedly upward. One of the porch posts was broken. The porch roof sagged and seemed ready to fall down.

The children cautiously stepped on the rickety porch. Henry pushed on the front door. It creaked open on rusty hinges.

CHAPTER 6

The Phone Call

"This place looks like our boxcar," Benny remarked as he stepped inside the cabin.

"It does!" Violet agreed. "It's got a shelf with dishes, same as our boxcar."

"Only we didn't have a fireplace," Henry said.

"Our boxcar was cleaner, too," Jessie added. Cobwebs draped the rafters and the plank floor was littered with leaves. The place needed a good sweeping!

"I wonder who lived here," Henry said, wiping a circle of dust from the single window.

Benny was exploring the stone fireplace. He stuck his head up into the chimney.

"Benny, get out of there!" Jessie scolded. "You'll get filthy."

"Hey, look what I found!" Benny said.

He came out from the chimney holding a long, gray strip of something. It looked like a piece of fragile, old paper.

"What is that?" Jessie asked curiously.

Henry took the strip from Benny. "What a beauty! It's a snakeskin."

Violet jumped backward, alarmed.

"The snake is long gone," Jessie assured her. "He just used the rough rocks in the chimney to help shed his skin."

Violet shuddered. "Let's go. Rachel isn't here. I don't think anyone has been here in a long time."

But Jessie wasn't so sure. As they hurried out the front door, her foot kicked a cane-bottomed rocker. Always neat, she bent to straighten the piece of furniture.

Her hand brushed a square of pale blue paper.

"Henry, Benny!" she exclaimed. "This looks like that gum wrapper you found in your room."

Henry examined the scrap. "It's the same brand of gum. And it's not dusty. Someone *has* been here. And recently!"

"Maybe it was Rachel," Jessie said. "She chews a lot of gum." But if Rachel had been here, Jessie wondered, why did she leave? And where was she now?

Back at the college, the Aldens hurried into the main office. Randy Merchant was manning the radio. He held the earphones cupped over one ear.

"Has Rachel been found?" Violet asked him anxiously.

He shook his head. "One search team returned for supplies, but the rest are still out there."

"We can take over," Henry told Randy.

"Great," Randy said, handing Henry the

earphones. "I have to set up the observatory for tonight."

"I forgot," Jessie exclaimed. "Tonight is the party."

"People from town will be here, too," Randy said. "Even if Rachel isn't found, the show will go on."

"Don't remind me," groaned a voice from the doorway. Mark Jacobs came in, looking rumpled. "I'm the narrator."

"How did the search go?" asked Randy.

Mark just shook his head.

"Tough break," said Randy as he left.

Wearily, Mark collapsed into a chair. "What a terrible day. No sign of Rachel. And my latest notes are missing from the desk in my room. I'm supposed to present my paper tomorrow and I don't have the data I need in order to finish it."

"Is it that important?" Violet asked.

"Yes, it is. I've been working all year on my big discovery."

Benny pulled the tattered snakeskin from his pocket. "You can show them this. I found it, but you can have it."

Mark managed a smile. "Thanks, Benny. That's a great specimen, but my discovery is in the field of astronomy." Mark ran a hand through his rumpled hair. "I can't help thinking how strange it is that my notes disappeared at the same time as Rachel. Did you kids know that Hazel thinks Rachel planned to leave? Some of her clothes are gone."

Henry considered this new information. It *was* odd that Rachel and Mark's notes disappeared at the same time. But why would she have taken Mark's notes with her? After all, she had no use for them.

"Is there anything we can do?" Jessie asked.

Mark smiled. "Thanks, but you're already helping with the search. And Hazel told me you're serving breakfast tomorrow. You don't have to worry about my troubles. All is not lost."

"What do you mean?" asked Benny.

"I keep a second set of notes hidden in the observatory. That set doesn't have my latest data, but it's a start," Mark replied. "I'm going back out to search for Rachel until dinnertime. Then I'll skip dinner and work on my paper at the observatory. And I'll be there tonight for the meteor shower."

A noise outside the door caught Benny's attention. It sounded like someone choking.

Mark stood up. "Got to hit the trail. My team should have fresh provisions by now."

As Mark headed out the door, he bumped into Eugene.

"*There* you are," Eugene exclaimed in an overly loud voice. "We've been wondering where you were. Our team is set to go out again."

"Wish us luck," Mark said.

As soon as the young men were out of sight, Henry said, "There's something weird about Eugene Scott."

"I think so, too," Violet agreed. "He acts like he's friendly, but he's really not."

Henry nodded. "You've hit the nail on the head, Violet. Eugene is a big phony. He pretends to like Mark, but he's really his rival."

"What's a rival?" Benny asked. He rolled his snakeskin neatly and placed it in his pocket. He couldn't wait to show it to Grandfather.

"It means they are in competition with each other," Jessie explained. "Like in a race."

Suddenly the radio crackled.

Henry sat up straight, pulling the microphone toward him. "This is Eagletop," he spoke anxiously into the microphone, remembering the code name. "Is anyone out there?"

After more squawks and static, a voice said, "This is A Team, Eagletop. It's getting dark. We're coming in. I've already signaled the other teams to abandon the search."

"Eagletop reads you," Henry said. "Over and out." Slowly he pulled off the headphones.

Dr. Porter came into the room. "I heard from the hall. You children have been a big help. My thanks to you."

Grimly, the Aldens left the main building. After cleaning up in their dorm rooms, they met in the dining room.

A steam-table buffet had been set up along one wall. Hot dishes gave off delicious aromas.

"Mmmm," Benny said, first in line as always. "Macaroni and cheese."

"Don't take more than you can eat," Violet advised him.

When their plates were filled, they headed toward a table. Grandfather was waiting for them.

"I'm going to dine with my grandchildren tonight," he said.

Just then Able Porter rushed up. "I have wonderful news! Rachel Cunningham just called."

"She did?" Jessie asked, astonished. "Is she okay?"

"Where is she?" Violet wanted to know.

Dr. Porter raised a hand to halt the questions. "She's fine. She's at her grandparents' house on the other side of the mountain."

"Why did she leave?" Henry asked.

"She would only say that she had personal problems," Dr. Porter replied. "And that as soon as she worked them out, she'd return to the college."

Grandfather poured iced tea for everyone. "This is very peculiar, Able. Why couldn't Rachel tell you before she left? We thought something had happened to her."

"I know," Dr. Porter agreed. "I told her about the search team. She apologized but wouldn't tell me anything more. But she sounded good. I'm so relieved she's okay."

Jessie wondered if that was true. She couldn't stop thinking about the gum wrapper she'd found in the abandoned cabin. Suppose Rachel had dropped the wrapper on purpose, as a clue? Maybe she had been kidnapped. Maybe her kidnapper forced Rachel to make that call to Dr. Porter.

Before she could voice her concerns, Grandfather said, "It's nearly time to go to the observatory."

"That's right!" Henry said. "Tonight's the shower."

"I already took one bath today," said Benny, joking.

The meteor shower was a big event. Students from Mountvale College hiked up the trail or drove up the mountain to the observatory. Families from the town rolled up in pickup trucks.

People set up lawn chairs or spread blan-

kets on the grassy knoll around the observatory building.

"We won't be using the telescope tonight," Randy Merchant explained as he led the Aldens and Dr. Porter into the dome room. "The best way to view meteors is with the unaided eye. They move too fast to track with a telescope."

Lawn chairs had been set up in rows around the telescope. Faculty members and special guests were filling the seats.

"Make yourselves comfortable," Randy told the gathering crowd. "Lie back so your neck won't get tired."

The Aldens sat down and tilted their chairs.

"I feel like I'm at the beach!" Violet said with a giggle. She claimed the seat at the end of the row, next to Randy's desk.

Randy pushed a button on the wall. The domed roof slid open all the way.

Stars glittered in the night sky. The show was about to begin.

CHAPTER 7

A Thief in the Night

Violet leaned back with a contented sigh. Stars lay scattered against the velvety black like diamonds. She felt like she was part of the soft summer night.

Benny sat up. "I don't see anything," he said. "Except outer space."

"You will," Randy promised. "Keep your eye on the sky!" Then he added, "By the way, I have the scoop on a terrific story."

Now Jessie sat up, interested. "What's it about?"

But Randy merely put his forefinger to

his lips. Then he left to join some other faculty members.

"Everybody's got a secret around here! I wonder what kind of a story he's writing," Jessie asked Henry.

"Maybe it has something to do with Eugene's and Mark's discoveries," Henry answered.

"But *those* are secret," Jessie said. "Mark and Eugene won't tell anyone about their discoveries until tomorrow." The next day was the last day of the conference. The young astronomers would present their papers to the scientists.

Benny scooted to the end of his lawn chair. For once he wasn't interested in the mystery. He wanted to see a meteor! "I haven't seen one single falling star," he complained. "Where are they, anyway?"

"Be patient," Henry told him. He was wondering if Mark Jacobs would make it tonight after all. He spied Eugene Scott sitting at the end of the front row with some other students.

Just then Mark rushed into the observatory. He carried a folder, which he placed on Randy's desk.

"Ah!" said Dr. Porter. "Our narrator has arrived."

"Sorry I'm late," Mark said, clipping a small microphone to his shirt collar. When he spoke again, his voice was amplified so everyone could hear him. "Welcome to my Perseid meteor shower. Actually, this show appears every year about this time. I can't really take credit for it."

The audience laughed.

"While I'm talking," Mark said, "please direct your attention to the east-southeast portion of the sky."

"That way," Henry whispered, pointing for Benny.

Mark continued his speech. "As you know, meteors are sometimes called shooting stars or falling stars. They aren't really stars, but particles of rock or metal. We see them as a bright streak when these particles enter our atmosphere and burn up."

"But they don't always burn up," Eugene put in.

"Right," said Mark. "Sometimes a fragment can strike the earth. These are called meteorites. Meteorites are usually small, like pebbles, but they can be large. Once, a meteorite hit a house in Illinois. It went through the roof of the garage, the roof of the car, and was found embedded in the front seat."

Benny had been staring at the sky so hard that his eyes were watering. Suddenly he saw a greenish flash.

"I saw one!" he cried, leaping from his seat.

"The first sighting of the evening goes to Benny Alden," Mark said in an announcer tone. "Congratulations!"

Benny was pleased. He bounced excitedly in his chair.

"There's one!" exclaimed Violet. "And another!"

"There's a whole bunch over there!" Henry cried.

At once, the sky was filled with streaks racing across the sky in shades of orange, yellow, and emerald green.

"I never knew there'd be so many colors!" said Jessie.

"The Perseid meteors appear to come from the constellation Perseus," Mark explained. "That's how they were named. They are dust fragments from the tail of a comet. Of all the meteor showers throughout the year, the Perseids are the most spectacular."

Jessie had to agree. The graceful streaks swooping across the sky were prettier than fireworks.

"How far away are they?" Henry asked Mark.

"Closer than you think," Mark replied. "Some are only sixty miles overhead."

"That's not so far!" Benny said. "When the next one falls, I'm going to go out and get it!"

Grandfather laughed. "Sixty miles is a long way to walk, Benny. And remember, Mark said most meteors don't make it to Earth."

But Benny wasn't discouraged. A meteorite would be a terrific souvenir to go with his snakeskin.

The show continued for another hour. The children tried to guess which falling star would disappear below the horizon first.

Violet found herself nodding off. It was so comfortable in the lawn chair. . . . Suddenly someone bumped the back of her seat. Whoever it was didn't apologize for jostling her chair. And it *was* dark in the observatory. Anyone moving around could easily stumble.

She settled back once more. Through half-closed eyes, she was aware that someone was near the desk. Then the figure melted into the shadows.

When she felt a hand on her arm, she jumped again.

"Sorry to startle you," Grandfather said soothingly. "But it's very late. You children should go to bed before you fall asleep right here."

"I think I was snoozing," she confessed, climbing out of the low chair.

Several people were getting to their feet. The meteor shower was nearly over. But a few were staying to look through the telescope.

In the lit hallway, the Aldens waited for Grandfather, who was discussing business with Dr. Porter.

Mark came down the hall, his folder under his arm. "Well, kids, how did you like it?"

"It was great!" Henry said.

"Tomorrow I'm going to go look for one of those meteor-things," Benny said, yawning hugely. "A whole bunch fell tonight. I ought to be able to find at least *one.*"

"You just might," said Mark.

"Did you finish your paper?" Jessie asked.

He tapped his folder. "In the nick of time."

As Eugene Scott walked toward them, Mark smiled at him. "Well, tomorrow is our big day. Good luck, Eugene." He stuck out his hand.

Eugene stared at Mark's outstretched hand. Reluctantly, he shook it. "Same to you," he said brusquely. He left without saying good night.

"He certainly isn't very nice," Jessie remarked.

Mark merely shrugged. "Some guys are like that. They're afraid somebody will steal their work or make a bigger discovery. I believe we should all work together for the good of science."

Henry admired Mark's attitude. "I think I'd like to be an astronomer," he said. "When you look through the telescope, you could see something nobody's ever seen before!"

"That's right," Mark agreed. "The possibilities are endless. You'd be good at astronomy, Henry, but it takes a lot of patience."

"What about me?" asked Benny. "Would I be good at it, too?"

Mark said with a laugh, "You'd be good at anything you set your mind to, Benny Alden!"

Benny puffed his chest proudly. "You hear that? I'd be good at anything!"

"Except going to bed," Grandfather said as he came up behind them, smiling. "I've been delayed, so you children go ahead to your rooms."

"I'll walk them down the mountain," Mark offered.

"I'd appreciate it," said Grandfather. "I'll see you all in the morning. Bright and early — it's the last day of the conference. And you all have a job!"

By now the rest of the spectators had left the observatory.

Mark led the way out the door. As he opened it, he dropped his folder. Papers scattered across the floor.

The children bent to help pick them up.

"Thanks," Mark said, stuffing the papers back into the folder. "I'll sort them out when I'm in my room."

Henry gave him the last sheet. "This one's blank," he said. "I guess it's an extra piece of paper."

Mark held the paper into the light, frowning. "I don't think I put any extra paper in here — just my document."

Quickly he spread the other sheets on the floor.

"They're all blank." Violet gasped. "What happened to your paper?"

Mark looked thunderstruck. He was speechless.

"Maybe you picked up the wrong folder," Jessie suggested. "Randy probably has a lot of folders on his desk. Let's go back and look."

They dashed back into the empty observatory. Mark flicked on the light switch.

But Randy's desk was neat. Only the sign-in logbook was centered on the blotter.

Henry checked around the desk, in case Mark's folder had slipped behind. He found nothing.

Mark moaned. "My work!"

"Maybe it was an accident," Violet offered. "There were a lot of people here tonight — someone could have put another folder on the desk and picked up yours by mistake."

But even as she said the words, she didn't believe it.

"Somebody must have stolen your paper," Benny said direly.

Mark nodded, like someone in a trance. "I'm afraid you're right, Benny. Someone stole my paper."

"But why?" asked Jessie. "Who could have done such an awful thing?"

"It could have been anyone," said Henry. "People were walking in and out all evening."

"The invitation wasn't just for the college," Mark said. "People from the town were here, too."

Jessie examined the stack of blank sheets in Mark's folder. "One thing is for sure," she said. "The crime was planned ahead of time."

Henry nodded in agreement. "The person was smart enough to bring blank paper to the observatory tonight. So he — or she — could leave it in Mark's folder as a substitute."

Mark's face crumpled with despair. "My notes were in that folder, too. My whole discovery is lost!"

CHAPTER 8

A Pale Blue Clue

The next morning, the Aldens reported to the dining room a half hour before the breakfast crowd.

Hazel Watson was waiting for them. "Good morning," she greeted. "I'm so thankful you children are pitching in."

"We're glad to help out," said Jessie.

Hazel handed the three older children aprons. A special pocket stitched on the front contained a small notepad and pencil. "Your uniforms," she said.

"Where's my uniform?" Benny asked.

"Remember? You and I are going to roll silverware in napkins. Let's see who can roll the most."

"Me!" said Benny.

A tray was pushed through the window that divided the kitchen and the dining room.

"Here are your breakfasts," Hazel told them. "Eat up, before the rush comes."

The children sat down and dug into bacon and eggs. While they ate, Hazel instructed the new servers.

"A pot of coffee and a pitcher of juice is on each table. Menu cards are already by each place. There are only three meals a diner can choose."

"Number one is the Mountaineer Breakfast," Jessie said, reading a menu card. "Hash browns, scrambled eggs, bacon, and toast. So if a customer chose that, I'd write *Number 1* on my notepad."

"Exactly!" Hazel said. "You will simply write down breakfast number one, two, or three."

"How do we know when the food is ready?" Jessie asked.

"And whose order is whose?" Henry wanted to know.

Hazel shook her head in amazement. "You kids are pros! After writing each order, bring it to me. When the food is ready, I'll call your name as the orders come up from the cook. The plates will already be on trays. Questions?"

"Yes," said Benny. "Do we get extra food?"

Hazel laughed. "You can have all you want when this is over! Thank heavens this is the last day of the conference." She held out her hand to him. "Let's go roll silverware."

The other three Aldens divided the dining room into sections.

"The tables have little flags with numbers," Henry observed. "So when you write an order, be sure to write down the table number, too."

By the time they had agreed on territories, it was eight o'clock. The first two diners entered the room.

They sat at table number fifteen, one of

Violet's. Nervously, Violet stepped up, order pad and pencil in hand.

"Our new waitress is very cute," said a student with a wink. Violet giggled. "I'll have breakfast number one." Violet wrote down *Number 1* very carefully.

His companion reached for the coffeepot. "I'll have the same. We heard Rachel's okay. Did she say when she was coming back?"

"No," Violet replied. "But we hope it's soon." Then she remembered to write *15* at the top of her order slip. Wouldn't it be awful if her customers' meals went to the wrong table?

Soon the trickle of diners turned into a regular stream. Henry, Jessie, and Violet scurried around, taking orders and delivering meals.

Violet was delighted that she got to serve Grandfather and Dr. Porter. Grandfather seemed proud of her.

One of Jessie's last customers was Mark Jacobs. He didn't want anything to eat, only juice and coffee.

"Mark looks terrible," Jessie commented

to Henry as they passed each other. "As if he's been up all night."

"He's so upset about losing his paper," Henry said. "It was his big chance."

Mark gulped the rest of his juice, then left. Jessie wished she could help him.

Eugene Scott was the last diner to straggle in. Though he was dressed nicely in a jacket and tie, the student's eyes were dark-circled. He sat down at one of Henry's tables and wearily rested his head on his arms.

Henry went over to the table. "Excuse me, Eugene. Are you having breakfast?"

"What?" Eugene looked around blearily. "Oh, yeah." He glanced at the menu. "Give me number three."

As Henry hurried off with the order, he passed Violet and Jessie. With the rush over, the pace had slowed. The girls were leaning against an empty table near the kitchen.

"What's wrong with Eugene?" Jessie asked. "He looks just as tired as Mark."

"He seems beat," Henry agreed. "But I can't figure out why. *His* paper wasn't stolen."

"That's right," Violet said. "In fact, all

Eugene does is brag about his discovery. He doesn't seem very excited, though."

When Henry left to deliver the order, Jessie kept an eye on Eugene's table.

First Eugene poured a cup of coffee. Then he pulled a pale blue packet from his jacket pocket. He unwrapped a small object and popped it in his mouth. He left the wrapper on the place mat.

Jessie grabbed Henry as he came by with Eugene's breakfast.

"See that piece of blue paper on his place mat?" she exclaimed. "I think it's a clue! Get it!"

With a nod, Henry went into action. He skillfully slid the plate of French toast in front of Eugene, while palming the scrap of paper. Then he left Eugene's table.

"Let's see it!" Benny said. He had finished rolling silverware. When he joined the girls, Jessie told him about Henry's secret mission.

Henry smoothed the small square. "It's a mint wrapper, not a gum wrapper! I wonder why he'd eat a mint before his meal instead of after."

"I don't know, but it's the same paper we found in our room!" Benny said.

"And the one Jessie found in the cabin," Violet added.

"The intruder ate mints," Jessie concluded. "Rachel chews gum, so it wasn't her. It was Eugene Scott!"

"But why did Eugene break into our room?" Benny wondered. "What was he looking for?"

"Something's wrong," Henry said, watching his customer. "He's hardly touched a thing on his plate."

Glancing around, Eugene dumped his French toast and sausage links in his napkin. He crammed it into his jacket and stood up to leave.

"What's he doing?" Benny asked.

Henry knew instantly. "He's smuggling food."

"To eat later?" Violet wondered. "As a snack?"

"He's taking that food *to* somebody," Jessie declared.

"We have to follow him," Henry said, shedding his apron.

"But we can't leave," Violet pointed out. "We're still on duty."

Hazel Watson came over just then.

"I believe that's the last of the breakfast crowd," she said with a relieved sigh. "You children did a fine job. I've heard nothing but compliments about our new serving staff!"

Jessie was untying her apron. "It was fun. Can we go now?" She noticed Eugene Scott through the window. If they hurried, they would still be able to follow him.

"Yes, you may," replied Hazel. "But there are lots of leftovers. You must be starved after all that work."

"No, thanks!" Benny said, practically running out the door. Right now, solving a mystery was more important than a blueberry muffin.

Once outside, the children looked in every direction. Eugene was nowhere in sight. He could have taken any of the trails that wound through the campus or up the mountain.

"We're too late!" Violet wailed. "We've lost him!"

Henry spotted another pale blue wrapper in the driveway at the base of one of the stone pillars.

"No, we haven't lost him! He left us a sign. This way!"

"I bet he took the secret trail!" Jessie said excitedly.

This time the children quickly spotted the faint trail that branched off the driveway.

"Doesn't that branch look broken?" Benny asked, pointing to a drooping tree limb on the right-hand path. "I bet Eugene did it."

"But we've been on this trail," Violet pointed out. "It could have been one of us."

"No, Benny's right," Henry said. "That's a fresh break. And the branch is pretty high. None of us is that tall. But Eugene is."

"Good detective work, Benny," Jessie praised.

Soon they saw more snapped branches

and stripped leaves. Despite the thick foliage and stinging insects, the Aldens hurried down the twisting path and into the glen.

The cabin door stood half open. Voices raised in argument filtered into the clearing.

"Stay back," Henry cautioned the others.

The children hid behind an oak tree and waited. After a few minutes, Eugene Scott appeared, carrying a folder. He stomped out of the cabin, rudely slamming the door behind him.

Muttering to himself, he found the footpath and quickly disappeared into the dense underbrush.

Henry stood up. "The coast is clear. Now let's see who Eugene was yelling at."

They ran up to the cabin porch and knocked.

None of the children was surprised when Rachel Cunningham opened the door.

CHAPTER 9

The Old Cabin's Secret

At first Rachel looked startled when she saw the children. Then her whole body slumped.

"I knew you'd come sooner or later," she said quietly. "You're smart kids. It didn't take you long to figure out where I was."

"We stumbled on this cabin a few days ago," Henry said. "It sure is hard to find."

"The cabin belongs to my grandparents. It's been in my family for generations. But when the land was bought by the college, my grandparents moved. They made the trail off-limits because it was too overgrown. They thought people might get lost. Hardly anybody knows it's here now." Rachel smiled. "You might as well come on in."

Jessie glanced around. Rachel's familiar pink sweater hung from a wooden peg. Paper plates overflowed the trash can. She could smell sausage from the smuggled breakfast Eugene Scott had brought.

On the table in the center of the room stood a typewriter.

"Dr. Porter said you were at your grandparents' house," Jessie said to Rachel. "But you've been here all along."

Rachel nodded. "I was there for one night but then I came here. Maybe the search teams covered this area when I was at my grandparents' house."

"Why are you hiding?" Henry demanded.

Rachel sank into an old rocker. "Make yourselves comfortable," she said. "It's a long story."

Benny and Violet settled on the hooked rug in front of the fireplace. Jessie and

Henry perched on the edge of the quilt-draped bunk.

"I don't know where to start," Rachel said, spreading her hands helplessly.

Henry pointed to the project on the table. "Why don't you tell us what you're doing. Are you writing a book?"

She shook her head. "That's Mark Jacob's science paper. Eugene and I are redoing it so it looks like Eugene wrote it."

The children were so shocked they could not say anything.

Then Jessie spoke. "There's a word for what you're doing."

"I know. Plagiarism," Rachel said, looking defeated. "It's just as bad as cheating."

"You're cheating?" Benny asked. He never cheated, not even at checkers. "Why?"

She brushed her bangs out of her eyes. "I'm not sure how I got in this fix. And I sure don't know *how* I'm going to get out of it."

Violet understood Rachel's distress. "Why don't you tell us why you're copying Mark's paper?"

"That's easy. For money," she replied flatly. Then, haltingly, she began her story.

"I've always wanted to go to college, but my parents couldn't afford to send me," she said. "So my grandparents scraped together a little money. I also got a job here, cleaning dorms and waiting tables."

"Are you going to be a scientist?" asked Jessie.

Rachel smiled sadly. "I hope to, someday." She went on. "Most of the students here have rich parents. I guess I resent them. I really resent the lazy ones, like Eugene Scott."

"If he's your friend," Benny said, "he's sure a grouch."

"He's *not* my friend," Rachel stated. "Eugene wants to be a great astronomer. He heard about Mark's discovery and wanted to discover something, too."

"So why didn't he?" asked Jessie.

"He's too lazy to do the work! Night after night, Mark would be up at the observatory. Once, Eugene tried to stop Mark from doing his research by changing the log. Mark had to reschedule. I've never liked Eugene," Rachel said. "And I'd never lift a finger to help him. But this spring the college raised their tuition rates. I needed money. And Eugene knew it."

"What did he do?" Jessie asked.

"He wanted to break into Mark's dorm room and find Mark's notes. Eugene was dying to find out what Mark had discovered. He paid me to lend him my key ring." Rachel's voice became soft and regretful. "So I gave him my keys one night."

Henry caught on. "It was the night of the cookout, wasn't it? Eugene broke into *our* room instead."

"I *told* Eugene which room was Mark's," Rachel said. "But he made a mistake and broke into the wrong room. By the time he figured it out, people were coming in from the storm. It was too late to search Mark's room."

"It gets worse," Rachel continued. "Eugene offered me even more money to make a copy of Mark's notes."

"And did you?" Henry prompted.

"I was so busy working at the conference this week," Rachel admitted. "But I finally got into Mark's room one night and made a copy of his notes."

"Was that the day you were really nervous?" Jessie guessed. She remembered Rachel dropping the tray at lunch.

"Yes! I spilled salad on your grandfather! I felt terrible, stealing from a nice guy like Mark. But was Eugene satisfied? No! He wanted me to write a draft of the paper! He offered me so much money, I couldn't say no."

She told the rest of the story quickly. Eugene concocted a scheme. Rachel would disappear so she could write Eugene's paper, using the stolen notes. Eugene joined the search party, even though he knew where Rachel was. He let everyone believe Rachel had truly vanished.

But on the day of the meteor shower, Eugene discovered that Mark had a *second* set of notes. He overheard Mark say he was going to redo his paper after the search.

Rachel went on. "Eugene figured Mark wouldn't let his paper out of his sight once he finished it. He expected Mark to bring his folder to the observatory. So Eugene had another plan. While everyone was looking at the meteors, he switched Mark's paper with blank sheets."

"I saw him when he left," Benny said, nodding. "His jacket looked lumpy."

"How could Eugene ever pass off Mark's discovery as his own?" asked Henry. "Surely Mark would recognize his own paper."

"That's right." Rachel nodded. "We stayed up all last night. We had to change some of the sentences so it would sound like Eugene's work."

"I still don't understand," Henry was puzzled. "Mark could just *say* that Eugene took his paper."

"But it would be Mark's word against Eugene's," Rachel explained.

She hung her head in shame. "In just a little while, Eugene will present Mark's paper and get credit for Mark's discovery. And I helped him do it."

Jessie stood up decisively. "Not if we hurry."

The other Aldens leaped to their feet, always ready to take action.

"What are you going to do?" asked Rachel.

Henry confronted her. "If we're going to get Mark's paper back, we need your help. You'll have to tell my grandfather and the others at the conference what you told us. Will you come with us?"

Rachel wrung her hands. "I don't know. It's only right, I guess. Why should Mark pay for my mistakes? But I'll be thrown out of school! My grandparents will be so let down."

"Not if you own up to it and tell the truth," Jessie encouraged gently.

With a sigh, Rachel reached for her sweater hanging on the wooden peg.

Just then they all heard a noise outside.

Benny thought it sounded like feet scuffling in leaves. He raced to the door in time to see Eugene Scott tearing up the path. The folder was tucked under his arm.

"It's Eugene!" he cried to the others. "He's been listening to us the whole time! And he's got the paper!"

The Aldens set out on the chase.

A fast runner, Henry took the lead. It was a tough uphill climb and he was surprised the heavier young man could run so fast.

Benny was right behind Henry. Being shorter, he could duck under bushes and take shortcuts.

In no time, Henry and Benny had reached the fork in the trail. The girls soon caught up and all four raced down the main driveway.

"What happened to Rachel?" Henry panted to Jessie.

"I don't know. I thought she was behind me and Violet. But she could have gone down another trail and got away. Rachel knows this mountain better than anyone." Jessie felt disappointed. Even though Rachel had helped Eugene cheat, Jessie believed Rachel had been about to do the right thing.

"There's Eugene!" Benny cried. He sprinted past the pillars and onto the campus. "He's getting into his car! He's driving off."

The children watched in amazement as Eugene spun the little red sports car past them and barreled down the mountain.

Henry shook his head. "I thought he'd run into the main building. That's where the conference is being held. He could still present Mark's paper."

"But he ran away instead," Violet said.

"He's probably scared of us," Benny declared. "Because we know what he did."

"Maybe," Jessie said doubtfully. "But Eugene seems like the type who can talk his way out of anything."

"And now he's run off with Mark's paper," said Henry. He squared his shoulders. "We still have to tell everyone what Eugene did. It won't get Mark's paper back, but at least he'll know what happened to it."

The children rushed into the main building and down the hall to the auditorium. Henry opened the door and they slipped inside.

The hushed auditorium was occupied by students. Grandfather was standing at the podium onstage, as if he was about to make an announcement. Several distinguished-looking men sat at a long table beside him.

Jessie nudged Violet. Mark was sitting dejectedly off to one side. How terrible he must feel, Jessie thought, knowing his big day was ruined.

"Let's go," she whispered to her sister.

Violet suddenly felt shy. There were so many people! "What are we going to say?"

"We'll just tell them what we know," said Benny.

"You know how grown-ups are," Violet pointed out. "They might not believe us." Several times in the past, the Aldens had discovered something important, only to be ignored by adults.

The door opened behind them.

"But they'll believe *me*," said a figure in a pink sweater.

Rachel Cunningham smiled, then led the children down the aisle toward the stage.

CHAPTER 10

Benny's Discovery

Grandfather's eyebrows raised in surprise as he watched his grandchildren and Rachel Cunningham climb onto the stage. They stood beside the podium.

"I hope this interruption is important," James Alden said.

"It's about Mark's paper," Henry said.

Mark sat up straight.

"We're aware Mark's paper is missing," said Grandfather. "What do you children know about it?"

This time Rachel spoke. "Everything, sir.

I told them. You see, I helped steal it. Eugene Scott paid me to take Mark's notes. We copied Mark's paper. Eugene was going to present it as his own work."

Mark leaped up. "What? Where is Eugene?"

"He's gone," Jessie replied. "We chased him, but he took off in his car. He took your paper with him," she added ruefully.

Rachel pulled an envelope from inside her sweater. "Not all of it," she said. "I still have Mark's original notes. Eugene forgot to ask me for them."

"That's why you weren't behind us," Jessie said. "You were getting Mark's notes."

By now everyone in the audience was straining to hear the onstage discussion.

James Alden spoke into the microphone. "I think we could all use a short recess." To Rachel and his grandchildren he said, "Let's go see Dr. Porter. This is a serious matter."

Silently, they filed out of the auditorium and down the hall. Dr. Porter's secretary ushered them immediately into his office.

"Now," said Dr. Porter. "What's this all about?"

Though she was clearly frightened, Rachel explained. She didn't make it sound like it was all Eugene Scott's fault. Jessie admired her for that.

"I know it was wrong," she said at the end of her story. "But I needed the money."

Dr. Porter frowned. "I'm sure something else could have been worked out."

"What's going to happen, sir?" Rachel asked.

"This college does not condone plagiarism," Dr. Porter said solemnly. "We cannot tolerate this kind of behavior."

Benny didn't understand everything the president was saying, but it didn't sound very good.

"We will find Eugene. If what you say is true, he will be expelled immediately," Able Porter pronounced. "What he did will remain on his records, no matter which other schools he applies to."

"And me, sir?" Rachel's voice wavered.

Dr. Porter shook his head with a sigh.

"I'm sorry, Rachel. You must be dismissed also. You were a part of Eugene's crime."

Rachel lifted her chin. "I understand, sir. I'll pack and be out of my dorm room as soon as possible."

"I'm sorry," the president told her sincerely. "I wish you had come to me. I would have helped your financial situation."

Jessie reached out and grabbed Rachel's hand. The young woman was trembling.

The meeting was over. The Aldens and Rachel left Dr. Porter's office.

Violet saw Rachel bite her lip to keep from crying. Violet felt like crying herself. She knew Rachel had done a bad thing, but the punishment seemed so harsh.

"Grandfather," she whispered, touching his sleeve, "can't you do something?"

"You mean to help Rachel?" He thought a moment. "Yes, I believe I can. Able Porter and I go back a long way. I'm sure he will work with me to help Rachel get a new start."

Rachel stared at him with huge eyes. "You mean I won't have to give up my dream of becoming a scientist?"

"You will have to leave Mountvale College," James Alden told her. "But I'm sure I can help you finish your schooling. The world needs young scientists."

Rachel threw her arms around him. "Thank you, Mr. Alden! I'll work harder than ever! I promise!"

"I know you will," Grandfather said. "Now, I'd better get back to the conference."

"Can I come, too?" Rachel asked. "There's something I have to do."

"All right," Grandfather relented. "Everyone might as well come. The conference is nearly over anyway."

Back inside the auditorium, Rachel went directly to Mark Jacobs. She handed him the envelope.

"I'm sorry," she said. "I hope you don't hate me, but I don't blame you if you do. Here are your notes."

Mark seemed overjoyed to get his notes back.

"I can rewrite my paper," he said. "And mail it to the conference committee. It'll be submitted late, but it won't be a total loss."

Then he said to Rachel, "No, I don't hate you."

Now James Alden stepped up to the podium. "Since you have your notes, Mark, why don't you give us an overview of your discovery."

Mark jumped up. "I can do that! I even have slides."

Henry poked Jessie. "We're finally going to find out Mark's discovery!"

The lights were dimmed and the projector was turned on. Everyone stared at the white screen onstage.

Mark took over the microphone. When he spoke, his voice vibrated with energy.

"In this great universe of ours," he said, "there are many wonders. Astronomers have always searched for those wonders, like the discovery of our own solar system. But lately astronomers are looking beyond our solar system. They are finding other solar systems, other galaxies."

He paused to click the button on the slide projector. A dark picture with a lot of dots came into focus.

"What is that?" Benny whispered to Violet.

"Shhh," she said. "He'll tell us."

Mark continued. "But I believe there are many wonders in our own solar system we haven't yet found. You all know about the asteroid belt that lies between the orbits of Jupiter and Mars. These tiny fragments orbit the sun just as the other planets make that journey."

Now Benny scratched his head. "What's an asteroid?"

Mark smiled at the youngest members of his audience. "Asteroids are pieces of old moons or planets. They may have come from a single planet that blew up long ago."

"Neat!" said Benny.

"They are only a few hundred miles wide. Some are only fifty miles across," Mark explained. "Most people find the asteroids boring. Chunks of rock that go around and around. Big deal!"

He clicked the projector button and a new slide came into view.

Now the audience stared at a picture of

dark space. Among the stars, there was a single fuzzy dot.

Mark used a pointer to tap the dot on the screen. "That, gentlemen, is my discovery. A new asteroid. It orbits *outside* the belt between Jupiter and Mars. It has a wobbly path. I think it's influenced by the orbit of our own planet, Earth. It's not the biggest asteroid, but it's not so small, either!"

There was a brief silence. Then the applause started.

The men at the table got up to shake Mark's hand. Grandfather clapped Mark on the back.

Mark stepped up to the microphone again. "I have one more thing to add. As you know, the International Astronomical Union oversees the naming of celestial objects. If I can get their approval, my discovery will be named the Alden Asteroid."

Violet bounced in her seat. This was incredible!

Jessie was overcome with excitement. "Did you hear that, Benny? We have our very own asteroid!"

"Terrific," he said, flatly.

The conference was adjourned.

Everyone walked outside.

Randy Merchant caught up to the Aldens. "Hey, guys!" he cried. "I can tell you *my* secret now! A science magazine has agreed to publish my article about young astronomers."

"That's great!" said Henry. Then he noticed a small device inside Randy's left ear. Randy Merchant had trouble hearing, he realized. No wonder Randy didn't answer his questions about the old trail. Henry was probably speaking into the wrong ear.

James Alden turned to Mark. "Thank you very much for naming your discovery after my family. It's a great honor."

"Your grandchildren deserve it," Mark said warmly. "Without their help, I wouldn't have been on that stage today."

"Now when we look up at the sky," Henry said, "we will know a little piece of it is named after us."

"Rachel," said Grandfather, "let's go talk to Dr. Porter about your future."

Rachel grasped Jessie's hand. "Thanks for being such a dear friend."

Jessie smiled back. She knew Rachel was a good person.

Mark and the children strolled down to the creek.

Benny squatted on the sandbar. His fleet of leaf boats was still docked. He launched one into the swirling water.

Mark knelt beside him. "You seem quiet, Benny. Aren't you excited about the Alden Asteroid?"

"Yeah, I guess." Benny pushed another boat into the current.

"Didn't you learn a lot about outer space this week?" Violet asked her little brother. It wasn't like him to be so unenthusiastic.

He sat back on his heels. "Well, I learned stars make pictures. But I really wanted to find one of those meteor-things. You know, to go with my snakeskin."

"A meteorite." Mark nodded, understanding. "You'd like an outer-space souvenir."

"Yes!" Then Benny's face fell. "But I didn't find one. I don't even know what one looks like."

Mark picked up a white pebble washed smooth by the water. He put it in Benny's hand.

"There," he said, "is your outer-space souvenir."

Benny stared at the rock. "Is this a meteorite?"

"No, it's just an ordinary Earth rock," Mark replied. "A piece of our planet."

Henry helped explain. "You see, Benny, our earth is part of the universe. We're in outer space ourselves."

"It doesn't feel like it," said Benny.

"That's because it seems like we're not moving," Mark said. "But we are. The earth is always spinning around its axis."

"You remember, that's what makes day and night," Jessie said to Benny. "When our part of the Earth turns away from the sun, it's night."

"And when it faces the sun, it's day,"

added Violet. "We're moving right this instant, only we can't feel it."

Benny's face lit up. "I get it! We're in outer space!" he said in triumph.

"Exactly." Mark grinned.

Now Benny pulled the rolled-up snakeskin from his pocket. He smoothed it flat and set the white pebble next to it.

"My Earth outer-space souvenirs," he said proudly. "Aren't they great?"

Violet frowned. She wished Benny would get rid of that snakeskin. But in the dappled sunlight, the gray, papery strip revealed a pretty pattern. It really wasn't so ugly, after all.

Benny had figured that out all by himself.

Violet tipped her head back. Tonight, she would look up at Benny's "outer space" for star-pictures and orbiting planets.

And if she was lucky, she might even see the Alden Asteroid.

GERTRUDE CHANDLER WARNER discovered when she was teaching that many readers who like an exciting story could find no books that were both easy and fun to read. She decided to try to meet this need, and her first book, *The Boxcar Children*, quickly proved she had succeeded.

Miss Warner drew on her own experiences to write the mystery. As a child she spent hours watching trains go by on the tracks opposite her family home. She often dreamed about what it would be like to set up housekeeping in a caboose or freight car — the situation the Alden children find themselves in.

When Miss Warner received requests for more adventures involving Henry, Jessie, Violet, and Benny Alden, she began additional stories. In each, she chose a special setting and introduced unusual or eccentric characters who liked the unpredictable.

While the mystery element is central to each of Miss Warner's books, she never thought of them as strictly juvenile mysteries. She liked to stress the Aldens' independence and resourcefulness and their solid New England devotion to using up and making do. The Aldens go about most of their adventures with as little adult supervision as possible — something else that delights young readers.

Miss Warner lived in Putnam, Connecticut, until her death in 1979. During her lifetime, she received hundreds of letters from girls and boys telling her how much they liked her books.